S0-BNE-847

vjbnf   VAL
363.325 MCCOY

McCoy, Erin L., author
Cyberterrorism
33410015458229   09/17/19

DISCARDED

Valparaiso Public Library
103 Jefferson Street
Valparaiso, IN 46383

The Top Six
/// THREATS
to Civilization

CYBERTERRORISM

Erin L. McCoy

Cavendish
Square

New York

Published in 2019 by Cavendish Square Publishing, LLC
243 5th Avenue, Suite 136, New York, NY 10016

Copyright © 2019 by Cavendish Square Publishing, LLC

First Edition

No part of this publication may be reproduced, stored in a retrieval system, or transmitted in any form or by any means—electronic, mechanical, photocopying, recording, or otherwise—without the prior permission of the copyright owner. Request for permission should be addressed to Permissions, Cavendish Square Publishing, 243 5th Avenue, Suite 136, New York, NY 10016. Tel (877) 980-4450; fax (877) 980-4454.

Website: cavendishsq.com

This publication represents the opinions and views of the author based on his or her personal experience, knowledge, and research. The information in this book serves as a general guide only. The author and publisher have used their best efforts in preparing this book and disclaim liability rising directly or indirectly from the use and application of this book.

All websites were available and accurate when this book was sent to press.

Library of Congress Cataloging-in-Publication Data
Names: McCoy, Erin L., author.
Title: Cyberterrorism / Erin L. McCoy.
Description: First edition. | New York, NY : Cavendish Square Publishing, LLC, 2019. |
Series: The top six threats to civilization |
Includes bibliographical references and index. | Audience: Grades 5 to 8.
Identifiers: LCCN 2018021918 (print) | LCCN 2018025450 (ebook) |
ISBN 9781502640437 (ebook) | ISBN 9781502640420 (library bound) |
ISBN 9781502640413 (pbk.)
Subjects: LCSH: Cyberterrorism–Juvenile literature.
Classification: LCC HV6773.15.C97 (ebook) | LCC HV6773.15.C97 M33 2019 (print) |
DDC 363.325–dc23
LC record available at https://lccn.loc.gov/2018021918

Editorial Director: David McNamara
Copy Editor: Alex Tessman
Associate Art Director: Alan Sliwinski
Designer: Ginny Kemmerer
Production Coordinator: Karol Szymczuk
Photo Research: J8 Media

Portions of this book originally appeared in *Cyberterrorism* by Jacqueline Ching.

The photographs in this book are used by permission and through the courtesy of: cover Lorado/E+/Getty Images; background used throughout Tflex/Shutterstock.com; p. background used throughout iulias/Shutterstock.com; p. 4-5 Elnur/Shutterstock.com; p. 7 Fiona Hanson - PA Images/PA Images via Getty Images; p. 9 Gorodenkoff/Shutterstock. com; p. 10 Ken Tannen/Shutterstock.com; p. 12 J. Pat Carter/Liaison/Getty Images; p. 14 Donat Sorokin\TASS via Getty Images; p. 16 Casimiro PT/Shutterstock.com; p. 17 Lee Woodgate/Ikon Images/Getty Images; p. 21 wk1003mike/ Shutterstock.com; p. 23 Craig F. Walker/The Denver Post via Getty Images; p. 25 TAK ISHIKAWA/Shutterstock.com; p. 28 Ann Hermes/The Christian Science Monitor via Getty Images; p. 29 U.S. Department of Agriculture/Wikimedia Commons/File:Freer Water Control and Improvement; p. District Diana Adame.jpg/cc-by-2.0; p. 30 adichrisworo/ Shutterstock.com; p. 31 Andrew Harrer/Bloomberg via Getty Images; p. 33 Peter Rogers/Newsmakers/Getty Images; p. 35 Ann Hermes/The Christian Science Monitor via Getty Images; p. 36 Nick Ansell/PA Images via Getty Images; p. 37 Barry Singleton/Shutterstock.com; p. 38 Robert Rosamilio/NY Daily News via Getty Images; p. 39 welcomia/ Shutterstock.com; p. 42 AP Photo/Mark J. Terrill, File; p. 43 Arjuna Kodisinghe/Shutterstock.com; p. 47 Aude/ Wikimedia Commons/File:Richard clarke.jpg/CC BY-SA 3.0; p. 49 Military Collection/Alamy Stock Photo.

Printed in the United States of America

CONTENTS

INTRODUCTION:
CYBERTERRORISTS ATTACK

The electricity goes out. You look out the window. The lights have been extinguished in every building for as far as you can see. You try to call emergency services, but the phone line is dead, and your cell phone can't connect to any towers.

You step outside in the hopes of learning what's happening from a neighbor or a passerby. A block down, on the main thoroughfare, hundreds of cars honk at each other and drivers gesture and yell or stand beside their cars. It's gridlock: all the traffic lights are out down every street. You walk to a nearby hospital, sure that someone there will know what's going on. Luckily, the hospital's lights are still on, powered by emergency generators, but things are far from calm. Medical personnel jog from patient to patient, jotting notes down on paper while tech specialists work frantically to get the computers—and the electronic health records that physicians need to assess their patients—back online. A virus seems to have corrupted the system.

You start to hear rumors whispered up and down the hall, between security guards and the police officers who have arrived to keep the

Opposite: We are all connected via a complex grid of electrical and communication services. If a cyberterrorist attack impacted this grid, it could affect thousands, even millions, of people.

peace, between doctors and nurses, between patients: a cyberterrorist group is behind the virus. It has also caused the power outage. Now that the whole city—maybe even the whole country—is vulnerable, what are they planning next? Suddenly, you hear an explosion. It shatters the windows of the hospital, sending glass flying. Is this, too, part of a multipronged terrorist attack? And without any way to communicate with the outside world, how can you decide what to do next?

WHAT IS CYBERTERRORISM?

When people think of cyberterrorism, this is the kind of scenario that is called to mind: a total systems shutdown. An unseen enemy. It seems like the stuff of Hollywood movies and sensational novels.

A terrorist is someone who, through intimidation and violence, seeks to communicate a political message or inspire panic and fear for political ends. Cyberterrorism utilizes the computers and technology that we rely on every day to achieve these goals. Not long ago, there was no such thing as a personal computer. Now, individuals, governments, and businesses alike can't imagine living without the electronic devices that keep them constantly connected to cyberspace. At no time in history has information been so accessible to the individual—or so vulnerable to attack by a single terrorist armed with just a computer and an internet connection.

Like anything of value, information can be stolen, corrupted, or destroyed. In spite of developments in encryption (protective coding), firewalls (barriers to unauthorized access), and other security systems, there is always the threat of criminals hacking through a computer network's security system from any location in the world, no matter how remote.

How likely is a widespread cyberattack that cripples not only an individual's computer or a company's network, but whole communities, cities, or even nations? Are we prepared? Is it possible to be prepared for such an invisible, undefined enemy?

REAL-LIFE ATTACKS

What makes the prospect of a large-scale, devastating cyberattack so believable is that hacking occurs regularly, often with apparent ease, and can inflict significant damage. Many hacking incidents turn out to be pranks. For example, on April Fool's Day in 2018, a self-styled hactivist (hacker-activist) known as Cyber Anakin hacked into a North Korean government website to link the page's Twitter logo to a false Twitter account claiming to be official, but actually designed to made fun of (and criticize) North Korea's leader, Kim Jong Un.

Gary McKinnon was accused (but never convicted) of committing the "biggest military computer hack of all time" in 2001 and 2002.

However, much hacking activity is far more serious, sinister, and potentially dangerous. A recent attack on the Colorado Department of Transportation sought a ransom in exchange for restoring access to two thousand computers. Luckily, the hack didn't take control of cameras or traffic signals—but it could have, said Srini Subramanian, a cybersecurity expert: "A cyberattack or threat could affect everything from municipal transportation to high speed transit rail that operates between cities … It could create crashes or chaos on the highways or even on city streets." In 2018, the United States claimed that Russia was behind the NotPetya malware, which sought to paralyze government agencies and businesses around the world and was "the most destructive and costly cyberattack in history," according to the White House. Russia had also allegedly attempted to hack the US power grid.

The hospital scenario that was described earlier in this chapter actually occurred to a lesser degree in 2017 (though the electrical power of hospitals was not affected). A global attack by ransomware called WannaCry affected some one hundred thousand organizations in at least 150 countries. It hit information technology (IT) and phone systems belonging to the United Kingdom's National Health Service particularly hard. They were locked out of their computer systems as the virus demanded they pay a ransom to access them again. A cybersecurity researcher brought a temporary end to the attack by activating a "kill switch" in the code.

How likely is it that such a disastrous chain of events will really play out, and how can we prevent this from happening? Are we too reliant on technology that may one day be used against us?

A 2018 poll found that 81 percent of Americans considered cyberterrorism a "critical threat." Allegations of Russian meddling in the 2016 presidential election had raised concerns over election cybersecurity. Could the results of elections be hacked? Other recent cyberattacks had threatened major global companies, organizations, and law enforcement. They had destroyed data and infected computers with viruses. Confidential data about billions of people had been compromised.

Ever since the terrorist attacks of September 11, 2001, Americans have been increasingly sensitive to and anxious about the vulnerability of the nation's computer systems. These systems are a tempting target that seems easily accessible to terrorists who could exploit them to achieve their destructive goals.

TERRORISTS AND FEARMONGERING

Terrorism is the use of violence by irregular combatants (those who are not members of a formal national army) to intimidate and frighten civilian populations and send a political message. It differs from traditional military tactics in one particular and very important way: civilians are

Above: It can be hard to predict where the next cyberattacker will strike, since their motives can vary widely and they can operate from anywhere in the world.

often targeted. Terrorists generally do not distinguish between civilians and military combatants. Civilians are seen as being active participants in and supporters of the power structure and social system to which the terrorists are opposed. They are seen as guilty parties, rather than innocent victims. In fact, terrorists often plan acts of violence that will result in mass civilian casualties.

The terrorist attacks of 9/11 are horrific examples of this. Most of the 2,996 people who died that day were civilians. The carefully coordinated attacks came with little advance warning. The attackers, members of the radical jihadist terrorist group al-Qaeda, were not part of any formal army, nor did they fight on behalf of any particular nation.

During the second half of the twentieth century, the United States had one primary and obvious enemy: the Soviet Union. However, following the end of the Cold War and the collapse of the Soviet Union, the

Smoke pours out of the North and South Towers of the World Trade Center in New York City after they were hit by planes flown by al-Qaeda terrorists on September 11, 2001. Both towers soon collapsed.

United States enjoyed a brief period of confidence and sense of security, believing that, because it was the world's only remaining superpower, there were no enemies out there who could inflict much harm. That illusion was shattered on 9/11. It turned out that the enemy was invisible, elusive, and able to strike any American citizen, territory, or installation in the world. Suddenly, no American felt safe—not at work, not on the street, not even at home.

AN INVISIBLE ENEMY

It's not hard to imagine scenarios in which cyberterrorism could be the perfect vehicle to create mass casualties and target civilians. Terrorists look for weaknesses that they can exploit. With the 9/11 attacks, it was the US air-transportation system and its lax security procedures. It is possible that the next weakness terrorists identify will be in one of our computer systems. Cyberterrorism gives them the anonymity they value, as well as the potential for massive damage and a huge psychological impact. "The next generation of terrorists will grow up in a digital world, with ever more powerful and easy-to-use hacking tools at their disposal," writes Dorothy Denning, a professor of defense analysis at the Naval Postgraduate School in California and a leading cybersecurity expert, in her article "Is Cyber Terror Next?"

It can be difficult to identify enemies who might use terrorist or cyberterrorist tactics. There are many nongovernmental militant groups similar to al-Qaeda. There are also domestic (homegrown) terrorists such as Timothy McVeigh, who bombed a federal building in Oklahoma City in 1995, killing 168 people, including nineteen small children in day care. Groups such as al-Qaeda and the Islamic State, a violent

In 1995, terrorist Timothy McVeigh bombed the Alfred P. Murrah Federal Building in Oklahoma City, Oklahoma, killing 168 people.

organization fighting for territory in the Middle East, already use the internet to spread messages of hate and violence. The threats are often nonspecific, but spreading fear through vague threats is a terrorist act. Terrorists' motives are not simply to destroy property but to cause psychological trauma.

Daniel Coats, director of national intelligence, named cyber threats as the number one threat against the United States in a hearing before the Senate Select Committee on Intelligence on February 13, 2018. "We face a complex, volatile, and challenging threat environment," Coats said. "Our adversaries, as well as the other malign actors, are using cyber and other instruments of power to shape societies and markets, international rules and institutions, and international hotspots to their advantage ... From US businesses, to the federal government, to state and local governments, the United States is threatened by cyberattacks every day." The challenge, Coats said, would be to maintain the latest and the best technology and technological ability in order to stave off such attacks.

Individual hackers, hacker groups, and organizations acting on behalf of foreign powers have all sought to probe the United States' cyber vulnerabilities. China has been accused of stealing intellectual property from US companies, Iran attacked and damaged Wall Street financial institutions in 2012, and North Korea allegedly hacked Sony Pictures. James Miller, former undersecretary of defense for policy, calls this "death by a thousand hacks."

Experience tells us that our computer systems are indeed vulnerable to attack. Security breaches have troubled the government for years. The National Cybersecurity and Communications Integration Center (NCCIC), which works to protect US communications and cybersecurity, discovered more than 194,000 new vulnerabilities among federal government members in 2017. There were 35,277 cybersecurity incidents in Fiscal Year (FY) 2017 (October 2016 through September 2017), 14 percent more than in FY 2016, according to a report to Congress by the Office of Management and Budget (OMB). Five of these attacks had such a powerful impact as to be classified as a "major incident." The OMB specifically reported 24,056 breaches exposing the personal information of hundreds of millions of people.

TYPES OF CYBERATTACKS

Documented cases of cybervulnerability and cyberattacks fall into one of six categories: flaws in the system, ransomware, cybercrime, hacktivism, cyberwarfare, and pranks.

FLAWS IN THE SYSTEM

Many cyberattacks take advantage of a preexisting flaw in a computer system, program, or piece of software. In 2017, a flaw in Apple's High Sierra operating system allowed anyone to gain access to a computer without even knowing its password. When developer Lemi Orhan Ergin discovered the flaw, he tweeted to Apple Support. The company wasn't apparently aware that there was a problem and didn't immediately know how to fix it. Such discoveries are not uncommon, however. Earlier in 2017, a security flaw in the Microsoft malware scanner actually made it possible for cybercriminals to use the scanner to install malware—software designed to disable or damage computers or computer systems.

Some hackers—even those with a history of operating malicious attacks—actually make a living as "bug bounty hunters." That's the case for Tommy DeVoss, whose home was raided by the Federal Bureau of Investigation (FBI) in 2002 after his hacking crew attacked Yahoo and government websites. Despite his conviction record, DeVoss now works

Ransomware can take control of a computer, refusing to relinquish that control until a ransom has been paid to the attacker.

to help companies find the security flaws in their computer systems. Agencies and companies paid more than $6 million in 2016 in exchange for the discovery of fifty-two thousand vulnerabilities.

RANSOMWARE

Some types of malware are designed to take control of, encrypt, or lock a computer and all its files. They then ask the victim to pay a ransom in exchange for restoring access. A prominent example of this was the WannaCry attack in 2017. Like so much malware, WannaCry took advantage of a Windows system vulnerability. Beginning on May 12 in Asia, it compromised computer systems, encrypted their files, and spread to 150 countries around the world in a matter of days.

It took international cooperation to fight back against WannaCry. The NCCIC coordinated with partners, researchers, and experts—including more than forty IT companies—around the globe to share information and determine the best method of counteracting the bug. Within five days, key alerts, reports, and advisories had been distributed worldwide. Regarding this type of collaboration, Department of Homeland Security assistant secretary for cybersecurity and communications Jeanette Manfra said, "I really believe that that's the model for the future."

CYBERCRIME

Cybercrime involves the use of a computer to commit fraud or theft, distribute obscene or offensive content, or engage in harassment. Obscene or offensive content is not always protected by the First Amendment of the US Constitution, which safeguards one's right to free speech. It includes written, oral, and visual forms of self-expression that are racist, subversive, or incite hate crimes.

The website WikiLeaks, which often publishes confidential information obtained by hacking, considers itself a hacktivist organization.

One example of cybercrime involved an eighteen-year-old New Zealander named Owen Thor Walker. He was the mastermind behind a cybergang that managed to infect more than one million computers around the world. Authorities said that Walker and his crew managed to steal bank and credit card information and manipulate stock trades. The botnet they released may have stolen as much as $20 million worldwide. (A botnet is a software robot that runs automatically. Botnets are usually computers that have been infected by internet viruses or worms and run malicious software that is controlled by the virus's creators.)

HACKTIVISM

Hacktivism is the use of computers to achieve social or political goals. Hacktivists want to protest or send a message, just as any activist does. Rather than march in the streets or organize boycotts and protests, however, they attack the websites of organizations they oppose. For example, antiglobalization hacktivists crippled the websites of the

World Trade Organization. Others, such as WikiLeaks, post often-confidential information online anonymously. However, many have questioned the strategies or motivations of some self-styled hacktivists, including WikiLeaks.

CYBERWARFARE

Cyberwarfare is the use of computers and the internet to conduct hostile acts, usually between two states. Many experts have claimed that China, Russia, and other governments have conducted cyberattacks against the US government and US companies—and point out that the United States, too, may be engaging in this type of warfare. The US government holds Russia responsible for a 2014 hack into Yahoo; and when more than a billion Yahoo accounts were hacked in 2016, experts indicated the attacks were carried out by "a state-sponsored hacker."

Although al-Qaeda and the Islamic State are not nations but militant terrorist organizations, their use of the internet to spread hate

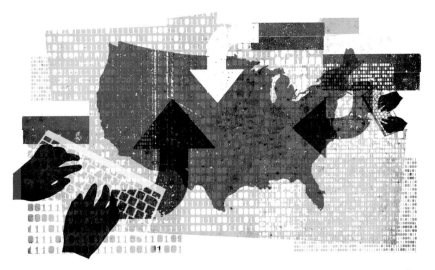

Hackers from all over the world have sought to infiltrate the US government's computer systems.

propaganda can be categorized as cyberwarfare. The Islamic State, also known as ISIS or ISIL, recruits many of its fighters online through sophisticated communication techniques and the dissemination of propaganda in the form of videos and other media. "Currently, ISIS is winning the online war," wrote military historian Andrew Byers and counter–violent-extremism analyst Tara Mooney in 2017. "We must begin to act rapidly and aggressively and beat ISIS at its own game."

Because so many weapons and military assets are connected to or controlled by digital tools, cyberattacks may now have the capacity to incite actual wars. As research group the Brookings Institution explained in 2017:

> There could be problems in the computer chips embedded in weapon system platforms; there could also be major vulnerabilities in critical infrastructure on which the US military depends for transportation and sustained logistical support. Disruptions to command and control capabilities that, in time of war, could leave military forces disconnected from each other—or [could be] falsely directed to shoot in erroneous directions or otherwise carry out inadvertent and harmful activities—could also result from various forms of sophisticated hacking.

In short, some hackers may be able to gain control of a nation's weapon systems remotely and hold that control for hostage, or worse, detonate the weapons.

PRANKS AND CHEATING

The last category of documented cyberattacks involves pranksters and cheaters who, though not usually a threat to national security, can still cause a lot of damage and disruption. Included in this last category were two California students, Tanvir Singh and Omar Khan. In 2008, Khan changed grades for a dozen students, including himself. Singh, meanwhile, had broken into the school to steal a test. Both pleaded guilty. Khan, who could have received thirty-eight years in prison if convicted on all of the charges against him, served just thirty days in jail and paid $15,000 in restitution. Singh was given three years' probation.

Even relatively harmless pranks can cost a person jail time. Kevin Poulsen was already a fugitive from the law for hacking into government and military security systems. In 1990, he heard that a Los Angeles radio station was giving away a Porsche to the 102nd caller. He made sure he was that caller by taking control of the entire city's telephone network. Poulsen received a three-year sentence for his crime.

WHAT IS A HACKER?

Many hackers are no more than curious amateur programmers. This was the case with "MafiaBoy," which was the internet alias of Michael Calce, a high-school student in Montreal, Canada. In 2000, he hacked into some of the largest internet sites in the world, including Yahoo, Amazon, CNN, Dell, and eBay. Calce launched denial-of-service attacks against these sites. Such attacks usually involve flooding websites with so many communication requests that the sites are overwhelmed in trying to respond to them. This results in very slow or unsuccessful loading of the sites for legitimate users. Often, the sites crash and are taken offline for a time. In court, Calce expressed the desire to move to Italy because of its lax computer-crime laws.

"Cracker" is another word describing a hacker who breaches computer security, whether to steal information, disrupt or destroy computer systems, support a political cause, or test his or her hacking skills.

Some hackers are computer-security experts who are paid by the government or private corporations to test their security systems by seeing how easily they can break in using various tools and techniques to avoid detection. Some of these security experts are former criminal hackers, or, like Kevin Poulsen, engage in criminal hacking during or after their legitimate employment.

Today, crackers have more and better tools and techniques at their disposal. Cyberattacks can involve these various forms of malware:

- **Viruses**: Malicious programs that arrive in file attachments and damage a computer's hardware, software, and files.

- **Worms**: Malicious programs that replicate themselves and travel from computer to computer by, for example, sending themselves to everyone in your email address book.

- **Trojan horses**: Malicious software that looks like legitimate software but, once installed on a computer, can delete files and destroy information.

- **Phishing**: Fraudulent emails or phone calls that seem like legitimate correspondence from reputable banks, social networking sites, and online auction sites. They seek to persuade you to provide sensitive personal information, such as bank account and credit card numbers, Social Security numbers, usernames, and passwords.

- **Control-system attacks**: Attacks on the computer systems that control a nation's infrastructure, such as dams and water supplies, electrical transmission networks, telephone and communication networks, and railroads.

Malware comes in a variety of forms and serves a variety of purposes, depending on the goal of the cyberattacker.

The Fight Against Spam

On December 16, 2003, US president George W. Bush signed the CAN-SPAM Act into law. It was the first national law to regulate the sending of unsolicited commercial emails, or spam. CAN-SPAM is an acronym that stands for "Controlling the Assault of Non-Solicited Pornography and Marketing." The law requires senders of commercial email to include a post office box or private mailbox and an "unsubscribe" link in all emails.

Canada has also enacted anti-spam legislation. In 2014, it became illegal to send a person commercial text messages, social media messages, and emails without their permission. A year later, installing programs on a person's computer without his or her permission was also outlawed.

THE CODE RED WORM AND OTHER CYBERATTACKS

One form of malware is the computer worm, which is a program that spreads by attacking other computers and copying itself onto them. The resulting flood of data can cause a performance slowdown or a complete shutdown of some parts of the internet. In 2001, a computer worm called Code Red infected the US Treasury Department's Financial Management Service (FMS). It deleted files and caused slow performance and system instability. The FMS was forced to pull the plug on its websites. As a result of the same worm, customers of Qwest, a telecommunications carrier, lost digital subscriber line (DSL) coverage for ten days. The White House's internet address was also targeted for a denial-of-service attack. The Code Red worm affected more than 750,000 computers worldwide.

In the wake of Code Red and similar worms, air-traffic-control systems, utility networks, emergency-response systems, and national-defense systems seemed suddenly vulnerable to crippling attack. Now that computer systems are involved in every aspect of our lives, particularly e-commerce (online banking, retailing, and networking), cyberterrorism has become a real threat to the economy.

The internet has millions of entry points and just as many infrastructure and software vulnerabilities. Yet its greatest vulnerability may be the human factor. Manipulating and deceiving people to gain confidential information is called social engineering. One master of social engineering was Kevin Mitnick, a hacker who eluded the FBI for two-and-a-half years in the mid-1990s. He broke into the computer systems of such top technology companies as Fujitsu, Nokia, Motorola, and Sun Microsystems. In his book, *The Art of Deception*, Mitnick wrote, "I could often get passwords and other pieces of sensitive information from companies by pretending to be someone else and just asking for

Kevin Mitnick spent five years in prison for hacking the computer systems of such companies as Fujitsu and Nokia in the mid-1990s.

it." He said that it is much easier to trick someone into giving you a password than to hack into the system.

It's no wonder, then, that 978 million consumers around the world lost $172 billion to online hackers and thieves in 2017, according to Norton, an online security company. What's worse, more and more damage is being done as governments and businesses struggle to keep up to speed with the latest viruses and malware.

In the twenty-first century, we are more reliant than ever on the internet and the technology that we use to connect to it. It's hard to imagine life without our smartphones, laptops, tablets, and e-book readers. As more and more of our household items become connected to the "internet of things," even our refrigerators, home-security systems, and thermostats can be connected to the web—and that makes them vulnerable to cyberattack.

ANTICIPATING ATTACKS

So much of the world is connected to and controlled by computers: banks, stock markets, the military, hospitals, electrical systems, nuclear power plants, and missile silos. It therefore isn't hard to imagine disastrous scenarios relating to computer-system vulnerabilities.

This fear is not irrational or misplaced. In fact, real cause for fear is increasing each year. "The United States was not routinely targeted by terrorists until 1982," writes Jonathan R. White in *Terrorism: An Introduction.* Since then, however, an entire industry has grown out of our fears of terrorism and attempts to defend against it. Cyberterrorism, in

Above: A cyberattack targeting electrical grids could cause widespread outages that could impact the economy as well as the safety of countless people.

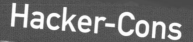

Members of a hacker team watch their system perform in the DARPA Cyber Grand Challenge at the DEF CON hacker convention in 2016.

Each year, hacker conventions take place around the world. Among the largest of these "hacker-cons" is DEF CON, which is hosted in Las Vegas, Nevada, and has an offshoot in Beijing, China. SummerCon is one of the oldest. Another, Black Hat, bills itself as "the most technical and relevant global information security event series in the world."

Who attends? Mostly computer security professionals, government employees, lawyers, and, of course, hackers. Anyone interested in computer code and design will find these conventions intriguing and worthwhile. Contests comprise a large component of many of these events. DEF CON urges attendees to organize contests that help teams prove and improve their technical skills.

particular, has become a growth area for think tanks such as the Potomac Institute for Policy Studies, which conducts research on issues of national security and the role of security consultants and IT specialists. As Dan Verton points out in *Black Ice*, an investigative look at cyberterrorism, no one could have imagined attacks like the ones on 9/11, despite the occurrence of earlier, smaller terrorist attacks such as the bombing of the World Trade Center in 1993. Even as cameras captured the first plane crashing into the World Trade Center on the morning of 9/11, people initially believed it was just an accident. In the same way, Verton warns, we may not recognize the looming threat of an imminent cyberattack.

Security experts try to anticipate when, where, and how a future cyberattack might occur. Perhaps terrorists might use a virus to snarl the taxpayer database of the Internal Revenue Service (IRS). Or as Richard Clarke, former White House advisor on cyberterrorism with the US Department of Homeland Security, has warned, they might tamper with the control systems of the power-supply infrastructure. They may then disable telephones and electrical power grids.

One of the difficulties facing security experts is identifying where a cyberthreat might come from. Although 9/11 turned our attention toward transnational terrorists, there has always been political violence in the United States' domestic history. If the country experiences a cyberattack, it is just as likely to come from homegrown American extremists, such as antigovernment militias, hate groups, or radicals supporting a particular political cause.

One such terrorist was Theodore Kaczynski. From 1978 until his arrest in 1996, Kaczynski, also known as the Unabomber, carried out a series of mail bombings that resulted in three deaths and twenty-three injuries. In 1995, he sent a letter to the *New York Times* in which he promised to "desist from terrorism" if the *Times* or the *Washington Post* published his anti-technology manifesto.

As history shows, terrorist attacks can come from unexpected places. That element of surprise—and the shock and fear that it creates—is one of the main tools that a terrorist uses. Even the most unlikely political causes and the least suspicious-seeming people can be at the root of violent and horrific attacks. For example, members of the Animal Liberation Front, a militant animal-rights protest group, have committed arson and other acts of terrorism. And in 2009, when thirteen people were fatally shot at a Fort Hood, Texas, military base, the culprit was none other than a US Army major and psychiatrist—Nidal Hasan.

Knowing where a truly destructive cyberattack will come from is as difficult as knowing where the next conventional terrorist strike will come from. It is also unclear if cyberattacks will be committed by well-known terrorist groups such as al-Qaeda or by an entirely new—and as yet unknown—breed of cyberterrorists.

ATTACKING CONTROL SYSTEMS

Many experts believe it won't take much for chaos to erupt. Most critical infrastructure in Western countries is networked through computers. In the United States, the control systems that connect and use these computers are known as SCADA (supervisory control and data acquisition) systems. They are obvious targets. SCADA systems are vital because they manage physical processes. They throw switches, shut valves, adjust temperatures, and regulate pressure. They are used in vital industries, including electric power, oil and gas refining and pipelines, water treatment and distribution, chemical production and processing, railroads and mass transit, and manufacturing. There are a growing number of connections between SCADA systems, office networks, and the internet. This makes them vulnerable to attacks.

Think of natural gas distribution. Computers monitor and control the pressure and flow of gas through pipelines. If a cyberterrorist who has hacked into the system instructs the computer to shut down the flow of gas, the pressure in the pipelines could build up to a dangerous level, causing an explosion.

Imagine that the computers of a major pharmaceutical company are the target. A cyberterrorist could tamper with the control system enough to interfere with the production process of a drug. The result would be a defective product, perhaps containing toxic levels of a drug. Or the product could contain too little of the drug to be effective against a patient's life-threatening illness. Then the cyberterrorist could tamper with the quality-control system so that such a defect would not be noticed.

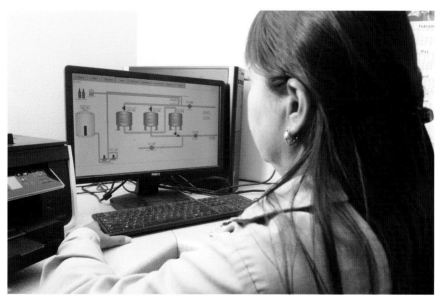

Diana Adame, manager of the Freer Water Control and Improvement District in Texas, monitors an arsenic-removal system via a computer interface.

A life-saving drug could be produced with the wrong levels of active ingredients, injuring or even killing thousands of people before the tampering is noticed. As more people learn what has happened, panic could quickly spread. In theory, any attack on the control systems of essential services—like water and fuel supplies, transportation, electricity, and health care—threatens public health and safety, and is therefore a threat to national security.

DISRUPTING INTERNET TRAFFIC

The internet's major hubs are also tempting targets for cyberterrorists. These are found in major cities where the equipment that collects and distributes internet traffic is located. A cyberattack on a major hub could disrupt internet functions and disconnect smaller cities linked to the internet via that hub.

Security experts worry that a malicious programmer might bring the entire web down with a botnet like Mirai, which made the internet unavailable to millions of Americans in September 2016 by attacking Dyn, a company integral to providing internet service in much of the United States. Repeated attacks flooded and shut down servers with malicious traffic. Disrupting communications in this way can make areas vulnerable to other types of attack, or can provoke dangerous panic among the populous.

MALWARE

There are many forms of malware, software that is designed to infiltrate and damage computer systems. They include computer viruses, worms, or Trojan horses. Spyware intercepts or takes partial control of users' interactions with their computer. Rootkits hide the fact that a system has been compromised. Crimeware steals money.

A single virus could disrupt our daily activities. Imagine if thousands of web pages suddenly went blank, only to be replaced by the error message "404 Not Found." Thousands of popular websites, from Facebook to YouTube, are replaced by malicious messages. Tens of millions of dollars are wiped off the share price of companies. News broadcasts start announcing that hundreds of thousands of personal bank accounts have been raided overnight. Soon, people make a run on their banks, angrily demanding their savings in cash. The rapid withdrawal of cash leads to a shortage of notes and coins. Meanwhile, the computer virus spreads to air-traffic-control systems, causing deadly midair collisions between passenger jets carrying hundreds of people each. By the time the virus is finally destroyed, thousands of people are dead. The country will spend years and billions of dollars repairing

404 ERROR

A 404 error message appears when an internet user attempts to visit a website but the link they have followed is dead or broken.

the damage and recovering from the devastation that was wreaked online and off.

These are some of the common scenarios that people think of when cyberterrorism is mentioned. Some experts suggest that these worst-case scenarios are quite possible, while others argue that they are just the product of overactive imaginations.

Of particular concern to some analysts is the possibility that terrorists might organize cyberattacks to coincide with violent attacks in the real world. When computers, electricity, or communications systems are down, people become more vulnerable to other types of attacks, and governments and the military may not be able to respond as quickly.

Are all the worst-case scenarios surrounding cyberterrorism really worth worrying about? The short answer is yes. In 2017, FBI director Christopher Wray gave the following statement before the US Senate's Homeland Security and Government Affairs Committee:

Virtually every national security and criminal threat the FBI faces is cyber-based or technologically facilitated. We face sophisticated cyber threats from foreign intelligence agencies, hackers for hire, organized crime syndicates, and terrorists. These threat actors constantly seek to access and steal our nation's classified information, trade secrets, technology, and ideas—all of which are of great importance to our national and economic security. They seek to strike our critical infrastructure and to harm our economy.

What's worse, Wray said, is that cyber threats are becoming harder to investigate because of the degree of anonymity the internet affords and because of the growing sophistication of such threats.

Above: A Chinese newspaper reports the April, 4, 2001, mid-air collision of an American EP-3 spy plane with a Chinese war plane.

FBI director Christopher Wray warns the Senate Homeland Security and Government Affairs Committee about cyberattacks in a 2017 hearing.

WHAT IS CYBERTERRORISM?

The number of breaches and attacks on US computer systems is increasing. Meanwhile, the internet is more frequently being used for posting hate-filled, threatening messages, photos, and videos. There have also been cybercrimes that were politically motivated. Do these breaches really amount to cyberterrorism? That depends on your definition of cyberterrorism.

The FBI has defined cyberterrorism as a "premeditated, politically motivated attack against information, computers, computer programs, and data that results in violence against noncombatant targets by subnational groups or clandestine agents." Noncombatants are civilians, citizens who are not members of an army or militia. Subnational groups are terrorist groups or militias that are not officially sanctioned by any national government but operate on their own, often in violation of the law and against established governments. Clandestine agents are secret agents—spies or intelligence operatives who work for legitimate governments, rebel organizations, or terrorist groups. The FBI's definition of cyberterrorism stresses that for hacking, vandalism, and tampering to rise to the level of cyberterrorism, they must result in violence against members of civilian society—or at least pose the potential for violent harm.

Following the midair collision of a US spy plane and a Chinese fighter jet in April 2001, some 1,200 politically motivated cyberattacks ensued. Targets of these angry acts of retaliation and protest included the US Air Force, the US Department of Energy, and the White House. Other perpetrators defaced websites with pro-Chinese images or launched denial-of-service attacks. Although these actions did have a financial cost (in lost productivity, repairing the systems, etc.), there was no loss of life or threatened physical violence.

Ralph Langner, an expert in industrial control systems, discovered the cyberweapon Stuxnet. He is pictured here in 2011.

THE GAP BETWEEN FEAR AND REALITY

Amid all the fear of cyberterrorism, some people point out that there have been few actual reports of infiltration of computer systems resulting in violence or physical danger to humans. However, many point out just how easy it can be to achieve this.

The year 2010 saw the emergence of Stuxnet, the virus that *WIRED* writer Kim Zetter called "the world's first digital weapon." Stuxnet, rumored to have been built by the United States and Israel, attacked SCADA systems to create real damage in the physical world: it issued orders to industrial control hardware that caused some of Iran's nuclear centrifuge equipment to break. For years, many countries had been concerned that Iran was developing nuclear weapons, and US president Barack Obama was reportedly "eager to slow that nation's apparent progress toward building an atomic bomb without launching a traditional military attack," according to the *Washington Post*. But there was a

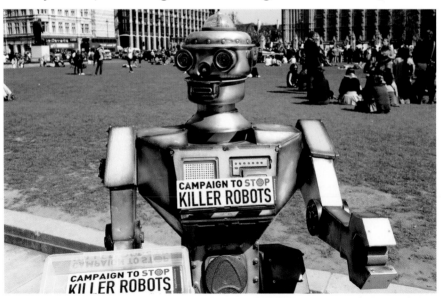

The Campaign to Stop Killer Robots, which argues that autonomous weapons should be banned, posted this robot in Parliament Square, London, in 2013.

problem: Stuxnet escaped the Iranian facility and started to spread around the world, threatening to do untold future damage. What's more, experts now warn that the release of such a weapon gives other nations and entities justification to develop similar technology. "Now there is a new weapon that can do a better job at destruction than bombs," wrote Paul Szoldra in *Business Insider*. "But the difference between highly-controlled nuclear materials and computer code is that anyone—and any state—can develop it."

Other experts, including such high-profile tech giants as Elon Musk and Steve Wozniak, have voiced concern over autonomous weapons—that is, robots capable of deciding who to attack. They have called for a universal ban on such "killer robots." While not many robots are used in warfare, some have been tested by the United States, including pilotless combat aircraft and undersea drones—but these still don't make decisions without human involvement. Many argue that this fear is overblown, and risks hindering the development of important future technology. However, others have put this concern to the test. In 2017, cybersecurity consultancy firm IOActive hacked a small home assistance robot and reprogrammed it to cackle evilly and stab a tomato with a screwdriver. They released a video of the hack on YouTube.

When it comes to hacking, an attack that could cause major damage and loss of life in the physical world would be challenging to achieve. Unless a cyberterrorist can hack into several major computer systems at once, seize control of large sections of a country's infrastructure and defense control systems, and unleash utter chaos in its water, energy, communications, transit, and weapons systems, the likelihood of widespread and massive death or injury is unlikely—though experts do disagree on this.

Experts believe that to pull off an effective attack on the nation's infrastructure, cyberterrorists would need to have more than just the ability to crack a computer system. They would also need to have enormous technical knowledge about, say, a plant's mechanical functions and how to exploit them. This is not information that is easily acquired. This argument goes back to the reality that it would be much easier for a terrorist to send a powerful message with physical attacks and crude explosives than through high-tech and expert sabotage. "Not only does [cyberterrorism] not rank alongside chemical, biological, or nuclear weapons, but it is not anywhere near as serious as other potential threats like car bombs or suicide bombers," said bioterrorism expert Dorothy Denning.

In a way, actual cyberterrorism has not caught up to the fear of cyberterrorism. In 1998, it was reported that the computers controlling the floodgates of the Theodore Roosevelt Dam in Arizona had been hacked. The hacker was a twelve-year-old boy. If he had opened the floodgates, reports said, walls of water could have flooded the cities of Tempe and Mesa, affecting nearly one million people. This is a terrifying prospect for sure, but the problem with this story is that it isn't true. It turned out to be an urban myth based on an actual, but far less dramatic, hacking incident involving an Arizona water facility and a twenty-seven-year-old perpetrator.

People have always had a distrust of computer technology—and when things go wrong, it is easy to imagine the worst. During the Northeast Blackout of 2003, less than two years after 9/11, many people immediately assumed there had been a terrorist attack. It was a widespread power outage that stretched through parts of the northeastern and midwestern United States and into Ontario, Canada.

A 1998 urban myth rumored that the Theodore Roosevelt Dam in Arizona had been hacked. If the floodgates were opened, two cities would have been flooded.

Even after the lights went back on, there continued to be incorrect media reports and internet speculation that foreign hackers were behind the blackout, as well as a second widespread blackout in Florida in 2008. Many of these rumors blamed Chinese government-supported hackers.

The power outages were actually caused by faulty, aging infrastructure combined with human error. The North American Electric Reliability Corporation, an organization of US electrical grid operators, investigated the 2003 blackout and concluded that a series of events contributed to the cascading blackout. First, the utility company FirstEnergy had failed to cut back trees that were growing onto high-voltage power lines in Ohio. When branches caught the power lines, they tripped. A chain of bad decisions and communication failures followed. Within minutes, much of the Northeast was plunged into darkness. This could easily happen again, with or without the help of cyberterrorists. A 2016 analysis by the Idaho National Laboratory found that, as the US electric sector continues

Times Square in New York City is plunged into darkness by the Northeast Blackout of 2003. Fifty million people in eight states and Canada were impacted by the blackout.

to incorporate more connectivity and networking, new vulnerabilities are arising, and state-funded hackers, including terrorists, are seeking to exploit these vulnerabilities.

Blaming foreign spies for these kinds of system failures shows how terrified Americans can be of the potential for cyberterrorism. Yet because our fear outpaces the actual incidence of cyberattacks, we are staying one step ahead of the game. We are remaining vigilant and putting defenses in place that help thwart or deter the very thing we are most afraid of. Indeed, to some extent, the apparent increase in computer crime is due in part to the fact that government agencies have improved their ability to detect and report breaches to computer systems.

CYBERTERRORISM OR EXPENSIVE NUISANCE?

Even hackers have a code of ethics. Most hackers, as opposed to malicious cyberterrorists bent on violent disruption and destruction, believe that cracking into a system for fun and exploration is all right as long as they

Blackout

The Northeast Blackout of 2003 was the largest electrical blackout in US history. It took place on Thursday, August 14, 2003, at 4:15 p.m. Eastern Standard Time. It affected approximately ten million people in Ontario, Canada, and forty million people in eight US states in the Northeast and Midwest. Eleven people died and total damages amounted to $6 billion. Power was restored in most places by the next day.

In order to avoid such disasters in the future, the US power grid is being continuously converted into a smart grid, which enables two-way communication between suppliers and consumers and increases the reliability of the system and its resiliency in the face of attack. It is also more energy-efficient.

don't commit a crime or cause any harm. Hackers often see themselves as free spirits and believe that sharing information is a positive thing and redistributes power. "Although hackers have the knowledge, skills, and tools to attack computer systems, they generally lack the motivation to cause violence or severe economic or social harm," Denning explains. According to her, "Attacks that disrupt nonessential services or that are mainly a costly nuisance" do not count as cyberterrorism.

Dire warnings of cyberattacks now seem like a regular occurrence. In the event of an attack, government agencies don't want to be caught off-guard, as they were on 9/11. As for security experts, they stand to gain from pointing out the vulnerabilities of the internet. Although the fear of cyberterrorism may be exaggerated, we can't afford to ignore its genuine threat. It is always a possibility that the success of the

Analysts work in a secretive government cyber-defense lab in Idaho. These analysts help to defend the country's power grid and communications systems.

West's "war on terror" can make frustrated conventional terrorists turn to unconventional weapons, such as cyberterrorism. As a new, more computer-savvy generation of terrorists comes of age, the danger seems likely to increase.

As technology develops and the skillset of malicious hackers grows, more and more damage is being done. In 2017, nearly seventeen million US consumers lost $16.8 billion to identity theft, much of it orchestrated online. This represented an 8 percent increase over 2016, and was a record high. As many as 6.6 percent of all American consumers were victimized. Millions, even billions, of people around the world have had their data compromised—and this raises questions about how many people a violent cyberattack could affect.

CHAPTER 4

FIGHTING BACK

Computer security company McAfee and the Center for Strategic and International Studies estimated that global losses to cybercrime in 2014 totaled as much as $575 billion. Given just how many people have already been affected by or suffered losses as a result of cyberattacks, it is reasonable to worry that more sinister acts of cyberterrorism might be on the horizon.

Disaster stories, dire predictions, and worst-case scenarios make great news. That's a big part of why we are so aware of the potential for tragedy. However, many security experts disagree with the idea that the next terrorist attack will come over the internet or through our nation's computer systems. Just as quickly as hackers can break into a system, security measures are being developed to defend the nation's computers. These defenses include firewalls (part of a computer system or network designed to block unauthorized access), antivirus software, intrusion detection and prevention systems, and encryption (security coding). They constitute the front line of defense against future attacks, and they are improving every day.

Above: An IT administrator installs a new rack-mount server. Security administrators are responsible for detecting weaknesses in a network.

SECURITY ADMINISTRATORS

A secure computer system should have an experienced security administrator. Many computer breaches and system accidents or failures are caused, at least in part, by human error. A well-trained security administrator can prevent such incidents. He or she runs tests to search for possible entry points and weak spots in a network. This way, the security administrator can stay a step ahead of cybercriminals. As soon as a vulnerable spot is identified, he or she applies the necessary patches to close it up.

A security administrator puts in place security policies that must be made known to, and strictly followed by, all personnel. He or she also sets up mechanisms that continuously test and evaluate the system and network security. For example, the system might run scripts— or lists of commands—every hour to report any suspicious activities on the network.

Sometimes, a computer system is connected to the internet as a trap. It appears to be part of the network, but in fact, it is isolated and unprotected on purpose. These are called "honey pots." Any breaches of this dummy system are monitored, and information on how a cracker gets in and exploits a system is gathered.

An experienced security administrator can spot false alarms, which may be triggered by legitimate system users during their everyday computing activities. Being able to quickly distinguish between an external threatening breach and an innocent internal user or system error can keep the security administrator from being distracted from genuine threats and attacks.

ARPANET

ARPANET is the predecessor of today's internet. "ARPA" stands for the Advanced Research Project Agency. It was developed by the US Department of Defense during the Cold War.

Some people think that ARPANET was designed as a central command system that would survive a nuclear attack. However, the real reason it was built was that there were only a few large, powerful research computers at the time, and they were separated by geography. ARPANET used a new technology called "packet switching" to link these far-flung, isolated computers into a network, allowing them to communicate and share information with each other. ARPANET grew to include email and file transfer. Eventually, it became a part of the emerging internet.

ISOLATING COMPUTER SYSTEMS

In theory, cyberterrorists could disable military, financial, and telecommunications systems. However, nuclear weapons and other sensitive military systems, as well as the computer systems of the FBI and CIA, are "air-gapped," making them inaccessible to outside hackers. Systems in the private sector tend to be less well protected, but they are far from defenseless.

When the Slammer worm spread around the world through Microsoft software in 2003, it targeted five of the internet's thirteen major hubs, and several major internet services and e-business providers were knocked out for almost two days. It also crippled two computer systems responsible for monitoring pressure and temperature during accidents at a nuclear power plant in Ohio. Slammer wasn't designed to target the plant. It more or less accidentally infected it as it spread from computer to computer nationwide. It is important to note that these two computer systems were not critical systems. They weren't part of the nuclear power plant's safety systems. In fact, the Nuclear Regulatory Commission requires computers that are part of safety systems to be isolated and inaccessible.

As cyberattacks increase and become more damaging, many have started to ask what real-world consequences they might have. A "Nuclear Strategy Review" released by the Trump administration in February 2018 included a provision permitting nuclear retaliation for nonnuclear offenses on infrastructure, including cyberattacks. The review stated that it "realigns our nuclear policy with a realistic assessment of the threats we face today and the uncertainties regarding the future security environment."

NEW INITIATIVES AND TECHNOLOGIES

That doesn't mean that officials aren't trying to stay one step ahead of cyberterrorist threats. One step that President Barack Obama took was to start a two-month cyberspace policy review in order to determine how well the US handles malicious hackers. One of the goals of this review was to identify new and improved cybersecurity strategies, as well as coordinate the security of military computer networks and develop offensive cyberweapons. In May 2009, President Obama announced the creation of a new "cyber-czar" position—officially called the cybersecurity coordinator—within the White House to combat what he said were constant attacks against American defense and military networks and more than $8 billion in losses related to cybercrimes committed against individuals and companies.

Under the Trump administration, there were rumors in 2017 that the office might be shuttered or reassigned to a bureau related to business and economic affairs. Former czar Michael Daniel warned that this wasn't a wise choice: "It's not just an economic problem," he said. Two dozen Congressional Democrats wrote a letter to the secretary of state making a similar argument: "At a time when the world is more interconnected than ever and we face constant cyber threats from state actors, it is vital that we retain a high-level diplomatic role to report directly to the secretary on global cybersecurity." The position was nonetheless eliminated in May 2018.

Richard A. Clarke served as cyberterrorism coordinator at the time the 9/11 attacks were perpetrated, and was the country's first de facto cyber-czar.

Numerous other security measures are being planned and implemented. Research and development is being done to create strong identification tools for computer control systems that are as successful as the Common Access Card, which employees must use to gain physical entry into sensitive facilities. For instance, better authentication methods for access to critical infrastructure are being developed, including digital certificates, smart cards, and biometric technologies like voice, retina, and fingerprint identification. A user would not be permitted to log on to a restricted computer or enter certain sensitive areas of the computer system or network if his or her biometric identifiers, when scanned, did not provide a match with that of an authorized user.

Following huge data breaches in the US Office of Personnel Management and the IRS, President Donald Trump issued an executive order in May 2017 calling for multiple federal agencies to take a careful look at their computer security systems. Key to improving security, according to the order, would be to update old technology, which is more vulnerable to hackers, and to train and hire more computer-security experts. In the case of a serious cyberattack or series of attacks, they would comprise the front line in a digital war. There is expected to be a shortage of 1.8 million such experts by 2022, likely because of a lack of educational resources and training in the field. This shortage may be one of the United States' greatest vulnerabilities.

OTHER STRATEGIES

Despite all of these high-tech initiatives and cutting-edge research and development, infiltration through the internet may be best handled with a low-tech solution. As President Trump's executive order acknowledged, training personnel in cybersafety is crucial. Furthermore, there are situations when it is better not to stop a hacker from breaking in. Instead, you silently track the hacker to see what his or her plan is, what his or her intentions or objectives seem to be, and where he or she is trying to go. In many instances, there is no need to even follow the intruder because it becomes clear that he or she doesn't intend to do any harm. Hackers are often just trying to gain free access to a computer and its network's communication resources.

Old-fashioned cooperation and community-mindedness can also help thwart a hacker or terrorist's malicious intentions. More than forty network providers that make up the backbone of the internet have agreements to help distribute each other's internet traffic in the event of a disaster. These companies are trying to improve their ability to reroute and reconnect data flow should a major provider be forced offline by a cyberattack.

A Louisiana National Guard Cyber Defense Incident Response Team member works with a local power company during disaster relief exercises in 2017.

Despite all the nightmare scenarios about cyberterrorism shared by government and intelligence agencies, antivirus software manufacturers, cybersecurity consultants, and internet conspiracy theorists, the actual threat of a devastating and crippling attack, while real, is not nearly as high as we are often led to believe. The fact of the matter is that actual reported instances of cyber infiltration have not been caused by terrorists, but rather ordinary criminals or "joyriding" hackers trying to cause mischief or access resources.

Still, vigilance many be the key to preventing damaging cyberterrorist attacks. Preventing such catastrophes is far better than mitigating their consequences. Fear, then, has been useful in motivating many security professionals and policymakers to take precautionary measures that have probably prevented a number of attacks already. Staying up-to-date on the latest threats and learning how to fight back remains the best way to stave off worst-case scenarios and keep people safe from cyberterrorism.

GLOSSARY

botnet A software robot that runs automatically.

breach To get past something's defenses.

cybercrime The use of a computer to commit fraud, distribute obscene or offensive content, or engage in harassment.

electronic health record Electronically captured data about a medical patient that can be shared digitally between doctors and hospitals.

encryption The act of converting data into code for security purposes.

exploit To use or manipulate to one's own advantage.

firewall Part of a computer system or network designed to block unauthorized access.

flaw A defect or weakness in someone or something.

generator A machine that converts one form of energy into another; a machine that can generate electricity when the usual electrical system goes down.

hacktivism The use of computers to achieve social or political goals.

infrastructure The basic physical and organizational structures needed for the operation of a society or enterprise, or the services and facilities necessary for an economy to function. The term typically refers to the technical structures that support a society, such as roads, water supply, sewers, power grids, and telecommunications.

intrusion The act of entering another's property without right or permission.

malicious Characterized by vicious or mischievous motivation or intent.

malware Software designed to disable or damage computers or computer systems.

manifesto A public declaration of one's intentions and/or ideas.

obscene Offensive to good taste.

perpetrator Someone who does something illegal; someone who commits a crime.

ransomware A type of malware that requires a victim to pay a ransom in exchange for restoring their access to encrypted files.

script With reference to computers, a list of commands performed by a certain program, often used to automate processes.

subversive Radically opposed to the government or society and the way things are done.

Trojan horse Malicious software that looks like legitimate software, but once installed on a computer, can delete files and destroy information.

virus A malicious program that arrives in file attachments and damages a computer's hardware, software, and files.

worm A malicious program that replicates itself and travels from computer to computer by, for example, sending itself to everyone in someone's email address book.

FURTHER INFORMATION

BOOKS

Krumsiek, Allison. *Cyber Mobs: Destructive Online Communities.* New York: Lucent Books, 2017.

LaVine, Howard. *How to Increase Online Security with Smartphones, Tablets and Computers.* Seattle, WA: Amazon Digital Services LLC, 2014.

Singer, P.W., and Allan Friedman. *Cybersecurity and Cyberwar: What Everyone Needs to Know.* New York: Oxford University Press, 2014.

Townsend, John. *Cyber Crime Secrets.* Amazing Crime Scene Science. Mankato, MN: Amicus, 2011.

WEBSITES

Cyberterrorism Defense Initiative

http://www.cyberterrorismcenter.org
This arm of the Federal Emergency Management Agency offers free training for those who want to learn how to fight cyberterrorism.

Office of the Director of National Intelligence, Information Sharing Environment

https://www.dni.gov/index.php/who-we-are/organizations/ise/about-the-ise
The ISE ensures that information is protected and shared responsibly by national security organizations within the federal government. This site offers important resources on how this is achieved.

US Department of Justice Computer Crime and Intellectual Property Section

https://www.justice.gov/criminal-ccips
The Computer Crime and Intellectual Property Section offers useful reports on intellectual property and computer crimes.

VIDEOS

Cyber-Terrorism and the 2016 Presidential Election
https://www.nbcnews.com/meet-the-press/video/cyber-terrorism-and-the-2016-presidential-election-585245763745
This roundtable discussion on the NBC News show Meet the Press discusses cyberterrorism's role in influencing the 2016 US presidential election.

Fighting Cyber Terrorism: Cyber Warfare Documentary
http://www.dailymotion.com/video/x30scbq
A US National Guard broadcast discusses how cyberattacks happen and the threats they pose.

What Is Cyberterrorism?
https://www.youtube.com/watch?v=cPTPpb8Ldz8
In this video published by the International Centre for the Study of Radicalisation, war studies expert Dr. Thomas Rid explains how cyberterrorism is defined.

ORGANIZATIONS

Canadian Cyber Incident Response Centre
269 Laurier Avenue West
Ottawa, ON K1A 0P8
(800) 830-3118
https://www.publicsafety.gc.ca/cnt/ntnl-scrt/cbr-scrt/ccirc-ccric-en.aspx
As part of Public Safety Canada, the Canadian Cyber Incident Response Centre is an organization that is responsible for monitoring threats, reducing risks, and coordinating a national response to any cybersecurity incident in Canada.

Information Systems Security Association International
1964 Gallows Road, Suite 310
Vienna, VA 22182
(703) 382-8205 (202) 324-3000
http://www.issa.org
ISSA is a nonprofit organization for cybersecurity professionals around the world. It offers education and publications designed to disseminate useful information on countering cyberattacks.

National Cyber-Forensics Training Alliance Canada

1455 de Maisonneuve Blvd West, EV7-640
Montreal, Quebec H3G 1M8
(514) 848-2444
http://www.ncfta.ca
This organization seeks to investigate cybercrimes perpetrated in Canada and encourage collaboration in order to achieve this.

National Cyber Security Alliance

1010 Vermont Avenue, NW
Washington, DC 20005
(720) 413-4938
https://staysafeonline.org
The nonprofit NCSA aims to spread awareness and promote education about cybersecurity and how individuals can stay safe at school, at work, and at home.

Oak Ridge National Laboratory

P. O. Box 2008
Oak Ridge, TN 37831-6252
(865) 574-8162
http://www.ornl.gov
The Oak Ridge National Laboratory is involved in the research and development of technologies to help in homeland security and national defense.

University of California, Davis Computer Security Lab

Department of Computer Science
University of California, Davis
One Shields Avenue
Davis, CA 95616-8562
http://seclab.cs.ucdavis.edu
The Computer Security Lab's mission is to improve the current state of computer security through research and teaching.

BIBLIOGRAPHY

Anderson, Nate. "Confirmed: US and Israel Created Stuxnet, Lost Control of It." *Ars Technica*, June 1, 2012. https://arstechnica.com/tech-policy/2012/06/confirmed-us-israel-created-stuxnet-lost-control-of-it.

Bannerman, Lucy. "Genius Who Wasted $1bn? My Son Gary McKinnon Was Just Looking for ET." *TimesOnline* (UK), January 13, 2009. http://www.timesonline.co.uk/tol/news/uk/crime/article5505489.ece.

Bergal, Jenni. "How Hackers Could Cause Chaos on America's Roads and Railways." Phys.org, April 27, 2018. https://phys.org/news/2018-04-hackers-chaos-america-roads-railways.html.

Bridis, Ted. "Senior White House Advisor on Cyber Security Confirms Resignation." *Channelweb*, January 31, 2003. http://www.crn.com/security/18822494;jsessionid=0BCZWZA4F-1MI4QSNDLPCKH0CJUNN2JVN.

Byers, Andrew, and Tara Mooney. "ISIS Is Winning the Cyber War. Here's How to Stop It." Hill (Washington, DC), March 21, 2017. http://thehill.com/blogs/pundits-blog/defense/325082-isis-is-winning-the-cyber-war-heres-how-to-stop-it.

Carafano, James. "Don't Kill the Killer-Robots—Just Yet." *Forbes*, August 5, 2015. https://www.forbes.com/sites/jamescarafano/2015/08/05/dont-kill-the-killer-robots-just-yet/#d-f68a3045690.

Cauley, Leslie. "NSA Has Massive Database of Americans' Phone Calls." *USA TODAY*, May 11, 2006. http://www.usatoday.com/news/washington/ 2006-05-10-nsa_x.htm.

Collins, Keith. "What You Need to Know About Trump's Executive Order on Cybersecurity." *Quartz*, May 12, 2017. https://qz.com/982128/what-you-need-to-know-about-trumps-executive-order-on-cybersecurity.

"Comprehensive National Cyber Security Initiative: Leap-Ahead Security Technologies." National Institute of Standards and Technology, February 1, 2008. http://www.nist.gov/public_affairs/ factsheet/cyber2009.html.

Cormier, Roger. "The 12 Biggest Blackouts in History." *Mental Floss*, November 9, 2015. http://mentalfloss.com/article/57769/12-biggest-electrical-blackouts-history.

Dacey, Robert F. "Critical Infrastructure Protection: Challenges and Efforts to Secure Control Systems." US General Accounting Office, March 2014. https://www.gao.gov/new.items/d04354.pdf.

Denning, Dorothy. "Is Cyber Terror Next?" SSRC.org, November 1, 2001. http://essays.ssrc.org/sept11/essays/denning.htm.

Elias, Marilyn. "Most Teen Hackers More Curious Than Criminal." *USA TODAY*, August 19, 2007. http://www.usatoday.com/news/health/2007-08-19-teen-hackers_N.htm.

Fidler, David P. "Transforming Election Cybersecurity." Council on Foreign Relations, Digital and Cyberspace Policy Program, May 17, 2017. https://www.cfr.org/report/transforming-election-cybersecurity.

Fox-Brewster, Thomas. "Prepare to Be Terrified—Watch a Hacked Robot Stab a Tomato with a Screwdriver." *Forbes*, August 22, 2017. https://www.forbes.com/sites/thomasbrewster/2017/08/22/hacked-home-robot-gets-stabby-with-screwdriver/#2b1f64d707a0.

Garamone, Jim. "Cyber Tops List of Threats to U.S., Director of National Intelligence Says." US Department of Defense, February 13, 2018. https://www.defense.gov/News/Article/Article/1440838/cyber-tops-list-of-threats-to-us-director-of-national-intelligence-says.

Greenberg, Andy. "The White House Blames Russia for NotPetya, the 'Most Costly Cyberattack in History.'" *WIRED*, February 15, 2018. https://www.wired.com/story/white-house-russia-notpetya-attribution.

———. "The White House Warns on Russian Router Hacking, but Muddles the Message." *WIRED*, April 16, 2018. https://www.wired.com/story/white-house-warns-russian-router-hacking-muddles-message.

Hein, Buster. "Huge Security Flaw Leaves Macos High Sierra Open to Attack." Cult of Mac, November 28, 2017. https://www.cultofmac.com/516365/huge-security-flaw-leaves-macos-high-sierra-open-attack.

"Identity Fraud Hits All Time High With 16.7 Million U.S. Victims in 2017." Identity Guard, February 9, 2018. https://www.identityguard.com/press-releases/identity-fraud-hits-all-time-high-with-16-7-million-u-s-victims-in-2017-according-to-new-javelin-strategy-research-study.

Institute for Security Technology Studies. "Examining the Cyber Capabilities of Islamic Terrorist Groups." Dartmouth College, 2003. http://www.ists.dartmouth.edu/library/164.pdf.

Insurance Information Institute. "Facts + Statistics: Identity Theft and Cybercrime." 2018. https://www.iii.org/fact-statistic/facts-statistics-identity-theft-and-cybercrime.

James, Michael S. "Cyber Attack Possible During Time of Terror." ABC News, September 23, 2003. http://abcnews.go.com/Technology/story?id=97157.

Keppler, Nick, Karen Freifeld, and John Walcott. "Siemens, Trimble, Moody's Breached by Chinese Hackers, U.S. Charges." Reuters, November 27, 2017. https://www.reuters.com/article/us-usa-cyber-china-indictments/siemens-trimble-moodys-breached-by-chinese-hackers-u-s-charges-idUSKBN1DR26D.

Kessler, Ronald. *The Terrorist Watch: Inside the Desperate Race to Stop the Next Attack*. New York: Crown Forum, 2007.

Lotto Persio, Sofia. "North Korea Has Yet to Notice It Got Cyber-Pranked on April Fools Day." *Newsweek*, April 12, 2018. http://www.newsweek.com/north-korea-has-yet-notice-it-got-cyber-pranked-april-fools-883789.

"'Major' Virus Incident at Barts and the London." ComputerWeekly.com, November 19, 2008. http://www.computerweekly.com/blogs/tony_collins/2008/11/major-virus-incident- at-barts.html.

Maza, Cristina. "The World's Best Hackers: Why Iran Is a Bigger Threat to the U.S. than Russia, China or North Korea." *Newsweek*, March 23, 2018. http://www.newsweek.com/best-hackers-world-iranian-cyber-spies-indicted-trump-859023.

Mission Support Center, Idaho National Laboratory. "Cyber Threat and Vulnerability Analysis of the U.S. Electric Sector." Energy.gov, August 2016. https://www.energy.gov/sites/prod/files/2017/01/f34/Cyber%20Threat%20and%20Vulnerability%20Analysis%20of%20the%20U.S.%20Electric%20Sector.pdf.

Mitnick, Kevin D. *The Art of Deception*. New York: Wiley Publishing, Inc., 2002.

Nakashima, Ellen, and Joby Warrick. "Stuxnet Was Work of U.S. and Israeli Experts, Officials Say." *Washington Post*, June 2, 2012. https://www.washingtonpost.com/world/national-security/stuxnet-was-work-of-us-and-israeli-experts-officials-say/2012/06/01/gJQAlnEy6U_story.html?utm_term=.608847b23c88.

National Defense. "Net Defense: Big-Bucks Cyber Security Program Proposed." Find Articles, April 2008. http://findarticles.com/p/articles/mi_hb6540/is_200804/ai_n25909474?tag=content;col1.

"NCCIC Year in Review 2017: Operation Cyber Guardian." Department of Homeland Security, National Cybersecurity and Communications Integration Center. Accessed April 24, 2018. https://www.us-cert.gov/sites/default/files/publications/NCCIC_Year_in_Review_2017_Final.pdf.

Newman, Lily Hay. "The Botnet That Broke the Internet Isn't Going Away." *WIRED*, December 9, 2016. https://www.wired.com/2016/12/botnet-broke-internet-isnt-going-away.

Ng, Alfred. "Bug Bounty Hunters Can Make Big Bucks with the Right Hack." *CNET*, October 13, 2017. https://www.cnet.com/news/bug-bounty-hunters-can-make-big-bucks-with-the-right-hack.

———. "Worldwide Ransomware Hack Hits Hospitals, Phone Companies." *CNET*, May 14, 2017. https://www.cnet.com/news/england-hospitals-hit-by-ransomware-attack-in-widespread-hack.

"Obama Begins Technology Security Review." BBC News, February 10, 2009. http://news.bbc.co.uk/2/hi/technology/7880695.stm.

Office of Management and Budget. "Federal Information Security Modernization Act of 2014 Annual Report to Congress, Fiscal Year 2017." Executive Office of the President of the United States. Accessed April 24, 2018. https://www.whitehouse.gov/wp-content/uploads/2017/11/FY2017FISMAReportCongress.pdf.

Poulson, Kevin. "Did Hackers Cause the 2003 Northeast Blackout? Umm, No." *WIRED*, May 29, 2008. http://blog.wired.com/27bstroke6/2008/05/ did-hackers-cau.html.

Reuters Staff. "U.S. Smart Grid to Cost Billions, Save Trillions." Reuters, May 24, 2011. https://www.reuters.com/article/us-utilities-smartgrid-epri/u-s-smart-grid-to-cost-billions-save-trillions-idUSTRE74N7O420110524.

Samuels, Brett. "Poll: Americans List North Korea, Cyber Terrorism as Top Threats." *Hill* (Washington, DC), March 5, 2018. http://thehill.com/blogs/blog-briefing-room/376729-americans-list-north-korea-cyberterrorism-as-top-threats-poll.

Sanger, David E., and William J. Broad. "Pentagon Suggests Countering Devastating Cyberattacks with Nuclear Arms." *New York Times*, January 16, 2018. https://www.nytimes.com/2018/01/16/us/politics/pentagon-nuclear-review-cyberattack-trump.html.

Szoldra, Paul. "A New Film Gives a Frightening Look at How the Us Used Cyberwarfare to Destroy Nukes." *Business Insider*, July 7, 2016. http://www.businessinsider.com/zero-days-stuxnet-cyber-weapon-2016-7.

Thomson, Iain. "'Crazy Bad' Bug in Microsoft's Windows Malware Scanner Can Be Used to Install Malware." *Register* (UK), May 9, 2017. https://www.theregister.co.uk/2017/05/09/microsoft_windows_defender_security_hole.

"2017 Norton Cyber Security Insights Report." Norton by Symantec. Accessed April 25, 2018. https://us.norton.com/cyber-security-insights-2017.

Uchill, Joe. "Obama Cyber Czar: Trump State Department Needs Cybersecurity Office." *Hill* (Washington, DC), July 26, 2017. http://thehill.com/policy/cybersecurity/344045-obama-cyber-czar-cyber-isnt-always-a-business-issue-so-state-shouldnt.

"US 'Not Prepared' for Cyberterrorism." *Independent Online* (NH), December 4, 2003. http:// www.iol.co.za/index.php?click_id=31&art_id= qw1070507887505S323&set_id=1.

Verton, Dan. *Black Ice*. New York: McGraw-Hill Professional, 2003.

White, Jamie. "Yahoo Says Breach Compromised Another 1 Billion User Accounts." LifeLock, December 15, 2016. https:// www.lifelock.com/education/yahoo-says-breach-compromised-another-1-billion-user-accounts.

White, Jonathan R. *Terrorism: An Introduction*. Stamford, CT: Wadsworth Thomson Learning, 2002.

Zetter, Kim. "An Unprecedented Look at Stuxnet, the World's First Digital Weapon." *WIRED*, November 3, 2014. https://www.wired.com/2014/11/countdown-to-zero-day-stuxnet.

INDEX

Page numbers in **boldface** are illustrations.

ransomware, 8, 13, 15
Russia, 8, 9, 17

SCADA systems, 28–29, 36
script, 44
security administrator,
    43–44, **43**
Stuxnet, 36–37
subversive, 15

terrorist, 6, 9–12, 17, 25,
    27–30, 32, 33–35, 37–42,
    43–44, 46, 49–50
threat, 6, 8, 9, 12–13, 19, 23,
    27, 30, 33–35, 37–38, 41,
    44, 46–47, 49–50
Trojan horse, 20, 30

virus, 5–6, 8, 9, 16, 20, 24, 27,
    30–31, 36

WannaCry, 8, 15
WikiLeaks, **16**, 17
worm, 16, 20, 23, 30, 45

ABOUT THE AUTHOR

Erin L. McCoy is a literature, language, and cultural studies educator and an award-winning photojournalist and poet. She holds a master of arts degree in Hispanic studies and a master of fine arts degree in creative writing from the University of Washington. She has edited nearly twenty nonfiction books for young adults, including *The Mexican-American War* and *The Israel-Palestine Border Conflict* from the Redrawing the Map series with Cavendish Square Publishing. She is from Louisville, Kentucky.